CONVERSATIONS WITH SHAMBHU

CONVERSATIONS WITH SHAMBHU

SUJATA SHARMA

Anecdote
Publishing House
For the love of quality reading!

Anecdote
Publishing House
For the love of quality reading!

anecdotepublishinghouse.com
champreaders.com

Anecdote Publishing House
2nd Floor 2/15 Lane no. 2 Ansari Road, Daryaganj-110002
Email: info@anecdotepublishinghouse.com
Website: anecdotepublishinghouse.com

Published by Anecdote Publishing House

First Edition 2024
ISBN 978-81-973806-9-3
MRP ₹ 299

Book Promoted and Marketed by Champ Readers Pvt. Ltd.
Edited by Meraki
Cover design by The Book Bakers
Layout by Graphic Tailor
Printed by Thomson Press (India) Ltd, New Delhi

For you, daddy!

Contents

Date: FEBRUARY 23, 2029 | Time: 7.30 AM

Where Is ADITYA?

"Aditya! Hurry up! The school bus will be here any minute!" Twenty-year old Pankaj was standing anxiously in the doorway and shouting loudly. In front of the doorway, a wooden plate inscribed with the names of his parents, Priyanka Kumar and Vivek Kumar in bold letters, was nailed.

It was a sunny February morning in the year 2029. The dreadful Covid Pandemic which had attacked the world had ended some years ago. The schools which had remained shut for almost two years had finally opened their gates for students all over the country in 2022. Though their lives had been greatly impacted by the Covid Pandemic, time had passed and everything had returned to normal.

Pankaj tapped his feet impatiently and shouted again "Adityaaaa!"

Despite his constant shouting, no one appeared.

Pankaj felt his nerves rattling with anxiety as he peered at the front door and then at the bus stop on the road where the school bus was about to arrive anytime.

Where was Aditya? Why had he suddenly become so lazy and difficult?

Dark thoughts came upon Pankaj as he recalled the days leading up to the pandemic. He was ten years old at that time and his brothers, Prakhar and Aditya were eight and six. Their mother, Priyanka, worked as a doctor and their father, Vivek, was a manager in a bank. The three brothers were raised by their hardworking, ambitious parents who valued teaching them the importance of competing and excelling at their studies.

The dinner time conversations in their family were mostly about the results of the boys' tests and who had secured the first position in the class. The boys had been appearing for various competitive examinations at the national level since they were in elementary school. Besides academics, the boys also competed in extracurricular activities like arts and music. Even the movies they watched, songs they listened to, were centered on the theme of excellence. They served as testaments to overcoming all obstacles, never giving up, and succeeding against all odds.

In this uber competitive atmosphere, the three boys grew up, becoming more and more like clones of each other every year.

Right since the beginning of their school, both

Pankaj and Prakhar were studious boys, always excelling in their academic work. They found their studies almost effortless as they sailed from one class to another. However, despite his best efforts, their youngest brother, Aditya, lagged behind.

Little Aditya was a naughty and imaginative boy whose eyes twinkled with mischief. His face looked like he was always ready to burst into merry laughter. His quick-witted, active mind was constantly coming up with fresh tricks.

Unlike his brothers, Aditya found his studies dull and uninteresting. He would struggle through most of the subjects, and would frequently receive bad grades that he would be ashamed to share with his family.

Then one day everything changed! The Covid-19 Pandemic arrived!

Due to the enforced lockdowns during the pandemic, all of them were forced to stay indoors. The family members had to divide their responsibilities to cope at home during those days. The children had to take online classes and study on their own.

It had not been easy for anyone, but it was hardest on the youngest member of the home, Aditya.

Aditya had initially been thrilled with the novelty of the lockdown. However, with passing time, he became gloomy and irritated. He did not take kindly to being separated from his friends and games. He detested attending online lessons and would not comply with the system. He began to have severe mood swings and would occasionally go through extended periods of silence.

The isolation due to the pandemic was expected to be of short period, but to everyone's dismay, it went on for a considerable amount of time.

With absolutely nothing else to do, Aditya finally turned towards his books. As he dusted them and started reading, he slowly developed interest and enthusiasm in his studies. He also made many friends on the Internet with whom he would chat about the marvels of science at all hours.

At last, the day everyone had been waiting for arrived. The schools which had remained closed finally reopened after the lockdown.

With the reopening of the schools, the biggest surprise was in store for Aditya's friends and teachers. They could not believe that the naughty Aditya that they had known before the lockdown had changed so much!

The old Aditya would avoid studying and find every excuse to get away from the classroom. He would also influence his friends to follow him in breaking every rule of the school.

But this new Aditya! This Aditya attended every class regularly; he was attentive at every moment. He amazed his teachers by submitting his homework and assignments on time. He scored very high marks in all the subjects, even in mathematics, which was a subject that he used to dislike earlier.

Mummy and Papa were ecstatic. All their dreams had come true! In an unbelievable stroke of luck, it seemed as if a magic wand had been raised, and lo behold! Aditya was transformed!

While everyone was busy celebrating his resounding success year after year, it was Pankaj who noticed that something was amiss. Aditya's performance in his school was undoubtedly good, but he had become a loner. He would always remain lost in his books, reading and making notes. When he was not studying, he would be browsing the internet to get ahead of his classmates. He did not want to communicate much with his friends. Though he continued being interested in sports, he limited it to football only as he was the school's team's best player. He wanted to prove that he was the best, and that's all that mattered to him.

Then gradually, this realisation dawned onto rest of the family members that Aditya did not look happy and agile like he used to before the pandemic had hit.

Pankaj tried talking with him many times but Aditya was reluctant to talk about it and would clam up.

One day suddenly out of nowhere, Aditya confided in his eldest brother. He told that the same achievements that used to excite him initially were now feeling repetitive. He felt listless, as if there was no challenge left in his life. The novelty of the situation had faded.

His enthusiasm and energy were slowly diminishing. Every morning he woke up with the realization that he did not look forward to the day.

Despite Pankaj counselling him, Aditya did not seem to feel better.

Aditya was sixteen years old now. One burdensome year had passed after another. With each passing year, Aditya had retreated further inside his shell. Now he had started missing school often, refusing to come out of his room. His attendance often fell short, but he did not seem to care about it.

All of a sudden, Pankaj's reverie was broken when he saw the familiar school bus ambling towards him. His heart sank. The school bus was here and Aditya had still not come out of the house.

As the bus doors opened, Pankaj took one last hopeless look at the house and shook his head. The students who had been waiting at the bus stand climbed into the bus. The doors closed and the bus bounced away in the sunrise.

As always, Aditya had been left behind.

Date: FEBRUARY 23, 2020 | Time: 7.50 AM

In The Pit Of Darkness

Ten minutes after the school bus left, Priyanka, Aditya's mother was knocking on the locked door of his room repeatedly.

"Aditya....," she called out.

There was no answer.

"Aditya....!" she knocked harder.

"Yes Mummy!" At last, a response came from behind the closed doors.

"You have missed the bus again." Her voice had a note of hopeless regret.

No answer again.

Priyanka was puzzled. What was wrong with this boy? What had happened to him? She and Vivek had always made sure that he got everything he asked for. One of the city's top schools with the best teachers! His parents and brothers supporting him, no matter what! When he asked for tuitions, he was provided with the best tutors! He had so many friends, both at school and near home! Everything was perfect. Then why did he behave like this?

Finding no answers, Priyanka lost her temper and shouted, “Aditya! Open the door!”

After a few moments which seemed like hours, the door finally opened and Aditya peeped out. His hair was unruly, standing up at every angle, uncombed. His eyes were dull and sleepy. He was still wearing the clothes that he had worn the day before.

When Priyanka looked at his disheveled state, she shook her head in disgust. She stepped forward and peered through the slightly ajar door and saw open boxes filled with stale pizza crusts on the bed. Discarded clothes and shoes were scattered all over the floor, along with empty Coke cans. The air of the room was stuffy and oppressive.

How did the boy breathe in there? Priyanka wondered.

“Get out of this room right now!” she shouted.

“Just a minute Mummy. I need to…,” Aditya mumbled incoherently.

“You don’t need to do anything! Just get out of your room so that I can get it cleaned. Go to your school before the gates get closed for the day,” Priyanka shouted back.

Yet, Aditya did nothing but stand there stubbornly while Priyanka continued to yell at him. Hearing the racket, Aditya's father, Vivek, came out of his room. When he saw Aditya standing there in that unkempt state, he also lost his temper.

"Why aren't you ready for your school yet?" Vivek's face was getting red with anger.

"Papa… I had to… I actually…," Aditya opened his mouth to speak, but he could not say anything that made sense.

"Get ready right now!" Vivek ordered.

In response, Aditya nodded, swallowed twice and scuttled inside his room.

Two hours passed and nothing more happened that day. Aditya did not come out of his room again.

After waiting for a while, Vivek and Priyanka got ready, ate their breakfast and with heavy hearts, departed for work.

In the car, Priyanka turned to Vivek and expressed her fears, "What do you think is happening to him? Is he under depression?"

Vivek frowned and shook his head, "Why would he be depressed? There is absolutely no reason for it! He has a good family, friends and the best school. He has everything that a child could ask for!"

Priyanka who had always been the more sensitive one, spoke again, "That's your perception. Who knows what he is going through?" Her voice was heavy with concern.

"What could he be going through? Everything is

perfect in his life." Vivek answered disinterestedly, his eyes on the screen of his phone.

At that precise moment, back home, Aditya was sitting on his bed, staring into space gloomily.

How could anyone know what's happening?

Even Aditya did not know what was happening to him. He had no idea why he did not feel like doing the normal things that he used to enjoy doing before. He had no clue why he was being pulled into a bottomless dark abyss. Aditya didn't feel like sharing his problems with anyone else. He felt that no one would understand him anyway.

At times, he had tried telling his brothers and parents. The results had always been disastrous. They would listen to him and start getting annoyed right away or give him advice which did not make any sense. His friends were too busy in their own world and remained clueless about his dilemma. Slowly, feeling misunderstood and confused, Aditya had sunk into a dark reverie of loneliness.

Date: FEBRUARY 24, 2029 | Time: 10:05 AM

Escaping The Shadows

Priyanka's phone had been ringing continuously.

She had been aware of the incessant ringing, but she was unable to attend to it. For many hours, she had been in the operation theatre, working on a complicated surgery. At last, an assistant came running and whispered something in her ears.

Priyanka frowned as she continued to work. Nothing could distract her from her work when she was in her zone. Though she kept operating on the patient in front of her, her mind was in a great turmoil by the news that she just heard.

As soon as she finished the surgery, she ran towards the doctors' room, changed her clothes and rushed out of the hospital building.

She started her car and made it race through the crowded streets of the city. As she drove, she thought grimly....

Aditya! Again Aditya!

This boy has been the source of constant trouble for a year.

This time it was a phone call from his school. The school Principal demanded that she should come to the school and take Aditya back with her immediately.

Aditya was being suspended from school!

According to the Principal, Aditya had misbehaved with a teacher in front of all the students. He was taken to the Principal's office, where he argued even more.

Priyanka sighed and thought, *Was there no end to the problems that he would give her?*

As her car approached the school, she saw two figures standing outside the gate. One was Aditya of course, and the second was the school Principal.

She parked nearby and walked towards them, her heart sinking. As she neared the gate, she saw another figure. It was a boy, wearing a blue shirt and blue jeans. His hair was unusually lustrous and was flying in the wind. Next to him, stood a golden colored dog with large floppy ears. They were both standing quietly behind Aditya.

Who was this boy? she wondered.

To her surprise, as she walked closer to the spot, she realised that the boy and the dog had disappeared. Only Aditya and the Principal were standing silently in an unhappy huddle, waiting for her.

"Where is that boy in the blue shirt who was just here?" Priyanka asked.

The Principal looked around and shook his head. "There is no one else, just me and Aditya."

"He was just there a second ago," Mummy said, pointing towards the gate.

The Principal shook his head again impatiently, "No one else is here, ma'am. It's just us."

Priyanka nodded. Yes, there was no one else. Was that just a figment of her imagination? Was her mind playing tricks on her?

Keeping aside that strange vision she had, she focused on the unpleasant task at hand. The Principal had already started launching into a volley of complaints against Aditya....

"...Aditya is either absent from the school or comes late in the class, with disheveled hair and dirty shoes. When the teachers pull him up, he either listens sullenly or speaks back rudely. And today, he crossed all the limits of decency. This kind of behavior is unacceptable in the school. It would set a bad example for other children. I am suspending him for a week. He must stay at home and introspect. "

The Principal went on and on, as Priyanka looked at Aditya unhappily. He looked back at her defiantly.

Priyanka just could not believe that her Aditya who had been such a bright and obedient student just some time ago, has changed so much. One of her children being suspended! This was so shameful! How will she face everyone now?

Where had her little, sweet child gone?

Who was this angry, defiant boy in his place?

Priyanka tried to persuade the Principal to consider relaxing the punishment. Wasn't suspension from school a bit too harsh? But the Principal would not relent. At last, defeated, Priyanka nodded and murmured an apology on Aditya's behalf. She assured the Principal that she would talk to Aditya and help him understand his misbehavior and get him back in an improved state. She knew that Aditya would not listen to her, but she made a promise to the Principal. What else can a mother do?

The Principal finally satisfied with the meeting, bid them goodbye. Priyanka and Aditya marched towards the parked car in silence. Soon, they were heading back home.

While driving, Priyanka glanced at Aditya. His face was scrunched up, with rage and humiliation. She wanted to say something comforting to him, but she held back. Something told her that if she spoke, there would definitely be an explosion, at the end of which Aditya will retire in his room for several days. She did not want to make things worse than they already were.

As the tense moments ticked by, Aditya gazed out of the car window with a sense of detachment. His eyes, weary and heavy, took in the familiar scene of the bustling city traffic. The world outside continued to churn relentlessly, each person caught in a frantic race to grasp something perpetually just beyond their reach.

At a sharp turn, he noticed a lush, green garden encircled by a white picket fence. How had he never seen this garden before? It seemed serene, tranquil and inviting to his exhausted spirit.

"Mummy, can you please stop the car?" Aditya spoke up.

Priyanka looked at him, startled, "What happened?"

"I just want to get down and sit in that garden for some time," Aditya insisted.

Priyanka first looked at the garden and then at Aditya.

"Why do you want to sit there?'

"It seems to be a new place. I haven't seen this before. Please, mom, may I just sit here by myself for some time? I'll feel better." Aditya pleaded again.

Priyanka was doubtful. Then she looked at Aditya's dejected face again. Finally she decided to let him have his way. "Alright. Sit here for a while. I will wait for you here."

"No Mummy! Don't wait for me. Please go back to your work. I'll come home myself." Aditya insisted.

Priyanka thought for some time, and then said, "Alright, Aditya. If that is what you want! Come home soon, as we need to talk."

"I will, Mummy. Don't worry. I'll be back soon." Aditya scrambled out of the car and walked away.

Date: FEBRUARY 24, 2029 | Time: 11.30 AM

Shambhu Arrives

Aditya walked slowly, towards the emerald green garden. It seemed as though he was being pulled by a powerful and mysterious force. It was something that he could not explain, but he just could not resist it. Something was calling him, and he had to answer it.

He walked on a path that was flanked by thick, shaded trees. Crystal-clear water drops were dripping from their enormous leaves. The air was fragrant with the scent of blooming roses. The melodious sounds of humming birds and woodpeckers were wafting through the entire garden. Squirrels with bushy tails were scurrying all over the path, making goofy eyes at Aditya. Vibrant butterflies and whirring dragonflies were flitting over his head.

Where had he arrived? Was it a paradise?

He kept walking for some time all alone in the park. There was not a single human in sight. At a distance, he saw a white bench under a dense tree. He made his way to the bench and sat down, looking up at the thick canopy of the trees.

For some moments Aditya remained seated with his eyes closed. He felt peace wash over him like gentle waves of the sea, soothing his troubled soul in the calm surroundings.

To this day, Aditya does not remember how and when he first became aware of the presence of another person near him. All he remembers is that when he opened his eyes, he almost jumped out of his skin as there was a stranger standing right in front of him.

It seemed as though the stranger had appeared out of nowhere. He appeared to be around Aditya's age; dressed in a blue shirt and blue jeans. A fluffy golden dog stood beside him, panting excitedly. Both of them were looking at Aditya intently.

For a long moment, the three of them stayed like that, just looking at each other, transfixed, not saying anything. The only sounds came from the water fountain nearby and the restless birds in the trees.

The silence was broken by Aditya, "Hi! What's your name?"

The boy said nothing, still looking at him intently with his big eyes.

Aditya attempted again, "My name is Aditya. What's yours?"

A small smile played peek-a-boo on that beautiful

face. "My name is Shambhu, and this is my dog, Bholu," he said, softly.

"Shambhu! What a beautiful voice you have! And… Oh my god! Is that a real snake around your neck?" Aditya looked aghast.

Aditya leapt and ran ten paces away. The snake around Shambhu's neck was sleek and beautiful, yet looked deadly.

Shambhu grinned in return, "Why are you so frightened? It will not hurt you."

Aditya was breathing fast, his heart beating at an alarming speed.

"Relax." Shambhu smiled again. "Look at you, you are not even breathing properly."

"How can I breathe properly in front of a snake?" Aditya spoke in a shaky voice.

Shambhu laughed, "But there will be lots of moments in your life when you will feel frightened and stressed. When that happens, will you stop breathing?"

In response, Aditya tried to breathe normally, inhaling and exhaling noisily.

Shambhu chuckled once more, "Not like this! You don't even know how to breathe! Let me show you how to do it."

He sat down on the green grass, signaling for Aditya to sit next to him. Aditya gave him a doubtful glance. Was this boy going to tell him what to do now? He hardly knew him. Then Bholu, the dog looked up at him with soft, liquid eyes and his heart melted.

What did he have to lose, anyway? He was just sitting in the garden, trying to kill time. He had nowhere to go, and no one to talk to.

He shrugged and sat down next to him. Bholu also joined them, panting happily.

Shambhu said, "First close your mouth. Now close your eyes. Now inhale mindfully."

"Mindfully?" Aditya was puzzled.

"That means, be present in the moment. Focus on the air travelling inside your nose, at the count of four. Now hold your breath at the count of seven. Feel the oxygen travelling inside your lungs and filling it. Now slowly exhale, at the count of eight. Keep repeating this."

"Inhale in four, hold for seven and exhale in eight seconds?" Aditya tried to keep pace with his words.

"Yes, four-seven-eight!" Shambhu repeated.

Both of them sat there, side by side, breathing together in tandem, in the same rhythm. The universe seemed to be filled with the sound of their rhythmic breathing.

"Remember Aditya! This is the first law of happiness. Breathing properly and mindfully! The most beautiful sound is that of your own calm breaths. Everything is possible as long as you are breathing."

Finally, Aditya opened his eyes. He felt an unfamiliar sensation moving through his body. All his muscles, starting from his face, to neck and shoulders, down to his back, and legs felt relaxed.

Aditya turned to look at Shambhu with new eyes. He marveled at this boy who seemed so sure of himself.

Shambhu looked at him and arched his eyebrows, "Now tell me, why are you looking so distressed?"

Aditya wondered if he could confide in a complete stranger about his problems. But then, he had never seemed to accomplish anything when he spoke to his friends. So why not!

"Let me start by saying that I have had the worst day of my life," Aditya shrugged, smiling sardonically.

Then he sat back, waiting for a dramatic reaction from Shambhu. He anticipated exclamations and enquiries.

Strangely, he got no response at all. Shambhu was gazing at a distant patch of blue sky thoughtfully.

Finally, Aditya spoke, "Aren't you going to say something?"

Shambhu turned to him, smiling mysteriously, "Perhaps it's a setup!"

"Setup? Setup for what?" Aditya looked at him, his mouth open with surprise.

"Indeed. The worst days are typically just divine appointments. They don't happen to just find you without any reason, They have a purpose and are fated. They are intended by a higher power to compel you to step beyond your comfort zone to think or do something that you've never done before. My friend, don't be so upset with the 'worst days'. You will never achieve anything that's meant for you without their help."

Aditya looked at Shambhu closely, deep in thought. It was not possible that this boy, who was just wandering aimlessly in this garden with his dog on a busy day, could possibly possess so much worldly wisdom. Yet, here he was, speaking the most profound words that Aditya had ever heard.

Shambhu patted his back, "Aditya, we will talk about what happened today… and also what has been happening over the years. But first, lie down on the grass with me..."

What a strange request! By now, Aditya seemed to be under a spell. Much to his surprise, he was obeying him as if he was hypnotised.

Aditya and Shambhu lied down on the soft grass next to each other, with their eyes closed. Bholu flopped down next to them and gazed at them with adoring eyes.

Beneath the foliage of the trees, the birds looked down at the two lads and their dog, contentedly stretched out on the grass. Vibrant coloured dragonflies whizzed past, dispersing the stardust of magic spells on their closed eyelids. A few raindrops drizzled on them, promising beautiful dreams. Aditya was transported to an exquisite world which was like a dream within a dream.

Date: FEBRUARY 24, 2029 | Time: 12:05 PM

Adiyogi

The minutes ticked by but Aditya had forgotten all sense of time. Finally, at the call of the blue jay, he opened his eyes and turned his head to look at Shambhu. His friend was smiling at him, his eyes twinkling like the distant stars. The snake around his neck had vanished. Bholu was sitting next to him, looking at the azure sky in front of them.

Aditya sat up and stretched his sore body.

"Shambhu, you appear to be just as old as I am, but you possess such wisdom. By the way, is blue your favourite colour? All your clothes are blue!"

Shambhu stood up and stretched lazily, "Yes, blue is my favourite colour. Adiyogi is also blue."

Aditya looked at Shambhu in confusion.

Shambhu gave him a disbelieving look, "C'mon Aditya! Don't you know who Adiyogi is?"

Aditya leaned on his elbow to prop himself sideways,

"No, please tell me."

"I suppose you must have heard about Lord Shiva?"

"Yes, of course, I have heard about him," said Aditya

Well, He is the one who is also known as Adiyogi."

"Oh! I had no idea that Lord Shiva is also called Adiyogi," Aditya confessed with awe and curiosity in his voice.

Shambhu continued, "Far, far away, in the mighty Himalayas range, towering mountain peaks stand silently beneath the clearest blue sky proudly. You might spot an odd eagle soaring high … but otherwise no sign of inhabitation. Among those mountains, there is one unique one… a grand, sacred mountain peak called Kailash. It's the Axis Mundi of Earth! That is where Lord Shiva resides, in deep meditation."

"What do you mean by Axis Mundi?" Aditya's analytical mind began to awaken.

Shambhu was staring off in a distance, as if his body was still here but his soul was on Mount Kailash, 'Axis Mundi', means the location where the earth and heaven converge, the home of Lord Shiva. He is the greatest mystic and the first Yogi. That is why he is called Adiyogi. He is also called AdiGuru, because he is the first teacher too."

"What did he teach?" Aditya asked.

"Everything! The understanding of the entire universe… the entire cosmos…and most importantly, the laws of living in contentment and happiness."

"What are those laws?" Aditya asked curiously.

Shambhu smiled compassionately at him, "My dearest friend, I am here with you for a few hours. I have to leave in the evening. Even if I want to, I can't teach you everything in the limited time we have. Understanding this knowledge is like diving into the deepest seas, and you can't know and understand everything even if you search for a lifetime."

"Ohh…" Aditya looked disappointed.

Shambhu looked at his dejected face and laughed, "Cheer up, Aditya. I will teach you five laws of happiness and the rest you will learn from your experiences and comprehension. I have already taught you the first law—to breathe mindfully. I will teach you the rest too."

Upon hearing this, Aditya cheered up instantly. He has found a friend and a Guru, who has appeared in his life out of the blue. What an unexpected and an amazing day it has been so far!

"So, shall we start?" Shambhu asked him.

"Yes, please!" Aditya was eager to begin.

The next moment, Shambhu was standing in front of him, holding two leaves in his hand, "Aditya, which leaf is more beautiful? This green emerald one, or the multicolored variegated one?"

Aditya leaned in closer, looking at the leaves carefully. He shook his head, "Both the leaves are beautiful, Shambhu, in their own unique ways."

"So if two different leaves can't be compared, can we compare two human beings?" Shambhu asked Aditya.

"No, not at all," Aditya replied.

"Then why do you constantly evaluate yourself with other people?" Shambhu chuckled at his naivety.

Aditya stood absolutely still, stunned at the realisation that Shambhu had playfully touched a nerve in him.

A distant memory that he had buried deep inside his consciousness flashed in his mind.

He remembered something that had happened two years ago when he had gone to school to find out the results of his final exams. Perhaps all of this had started since then?

Shambhu was looking at him, still laughing. He got an eerie feeling that Shambhu already knew everything.

Shambhu threw the leaves and said, "Tell me about it, my friend."

When I Felt Defeated For The First Time

In the morning, I struggled to get out of bed after a sleepless night. It was the day exam results would be announced.

As I sat drowsily in the car, a wave of fear and nervousness washed over me. My family expected excellent grades, as always, adding to my stress. A sinking feeling gnawed at me, fearing their disappointment.

The journey to school felt endless with my queasy stomach. My mother accompanied me to the school. When we arrived at the school, my heart sank as I saw the familiar school building looming large. It sank lower when I saw a huge crowd of boys in front of the notice board. My mother waited in the car as I navigated through a crowd of boys towards the result board. Despite the chaos, I managed to elbow my way through.

With tears welling up, I stared at my results in disbelief. Scoring only 65 out of 100 in Math seemed surreal. This couldn't be happening. Maybe I would wake up from this nightmare. Please, let it be a dream. I closed my eyes, praying desperately. When I opened them, nothing had changed. This was real!

For years, I had been one of the top students in my class, particularly excelling in Math, my favourite subject. This year, the course had become significantly more challenging. Many struggled to keep up, but I coped with the high difficulty level easily.

While my classmates grappled with integration and differentiation, I breezed through each problem. My Math teacher, Amit Sir, would shake his head at the other boys who would look back at him blankly. He often turned to me with pride, asking me to explain the solutions to the class. I would get up with a spring in feet, and walk confidently towards the board. As I would write down all the steps of the solution methodically, Amit Sir would nod approvingly.

This sequence of events repeated itself almost every day. I had started looking forward to those moments that made me feel the most sought after and respected student in the class. I started feeling a rush of power, that went straight to my head.

As time passed, I grew possessive of my elevated status in the class. I couldn't bear anyone outshining me. It shocked me at first, and I fought against it, but extreme competitiveness had silently taken hold of me.

Outwardly, I appeared so diligent and helpful that no one could have guessed that I had transformed into a self-

absorbed person who did not want anyone else to succeed. I had started deriving all my happiness from my superiority over other people. If anyone seemed to know even half as much as I knew, my heart rate would start racing with anxiety.

Then one day, everything changed.

As always, Amit Sir posed a rather challenging question on the board. Of course, I knew the solution. I sat back, smiling smugly and waited for Amit Sir to call out my name.

Then I heard Rishabh's voice behind me.

This was unbelievable! Rishabh stood up, asking Amit Sir if he could come over to the black board and write down the solution. How did he know the solution of this rather complicated question?

Much to my growing horror, Rishabh confidently stepped up and solved it flawlessly. He wrote the solution step wise, accurately and smoothly. Amit Sir was hopping around with happiness. His class seemed to be picking up, finally. He praised Rishabh effusively, patting him on the back.

My world shifted.

That night, I tossed and turned, listening to the endless ticking of the clock. I remembered the look of pride on Amit sir's face as he had praised Rishabh. That look used to be reserved only for me before that day.

From the next day onwards, I immersed myself in studying, but my motivation had changed. It wasn't love for Math driving me anymore; it was a bruised ego and the fear of losing my status. A dark terror was constantly pushing me, plunging me into a pit of insecurity.

I would spend more time trying to find out how Rishabh was faring with the assignments than on my own work. I would try to eavesdrop into conversations of Rishabh with his friends. I would stalk Rishabh on social media, completely absorbed with the activities of my self-appointed opponent. My own studies took a backseat as jealousy consumed me. I became someone I couldn't recognise, but I couldn't stop.

Now, standing before my dismal results, tears welled up. Rishabh had scored 95, while I, the former top student, managed only 65.

I heard a loud noise and turned around. Amit Sir had arrived and was hugging Rishabh. Some boys who were standing surrounding them were cheering for Rishabh loudly.

This moment should have been mine! These cheers should have been for me. This was simply not fair.

Unable to stand it anymore, I turned away, hiding my tears. I rushed back to the place where my mother was waiting for me in the car.

Anger boiled inside me as I screamed, "Can we just go home?"

Date: FEBRUARY 24, 2020 | Time: 12.20 PM

Stand Like A Mountain

Aditya sat on the grass, lost in the memories of the past. Finally he looked at Shambhu, wondering what his reaction would be.

Much to his surprise, in his reply, Shambhu tumbled on the soft grass and laughed with mirth. On and on, he laughed. He just would not stop laughing! Bholu started rolling in the grass with Shambhu as well, barking excitedly.

Aditya sat there, waiting patiently. At last, Shambhu stopped laughing, sat up and smiled at Aditya merrily.

"Look at your face, Aditya. It's a strange shade of purple! I knew that I had touched a nerve in you, but look how serious you have become!"

Aditya smiled and said, "So say something!"

Shambhu sat next to him and held his hand, "Aditya, my friend. Early that year, you were doing fine. You were working hard at your studies. You were listening to your soul. Your soul was seeking knowledge, and you were answering and fulfilling it. You were on the right path. But then in one weak moment, you let your ego take over. Do you know that your ego and fears are best friends? When ego knocks on your door, and you open it, then it does not walk inside alone. Along with your ego, countless fears walk inside too."

"And then?" Aditya questioned.

"Then your fears take over. They blindside you and make you lose your way. When your fears took over, you stopped working hard at your studies because then you started working hard at feeding your ego and answering the countless questions that your fears were asking you. That process consumed you, and you became directionless. But please understand that this is not your fault."

"Then whose fault is it?" Aditya asked, his eyes searching for answers.

Shambhu put an arm around Bholu, who had stopped rolling on the grass and was now lying contentedly next to him, "Nobody is at fault. It's just the way things are. You live in a socially structured module where everyone has to be first, exactly like each other. Once you are comparable, you must strive to be the greatest. We're all racing against each other. Those who follow this directive are rewarded. Anyone who dares to question it is humiliated and ridiculed to the point of depression and self-harm. Everyone is unhappy, even the one who finishes first in the race."

Aditya was chewing a blade of grass, deep in thought. "Tell me, how can I overcome this feeling of competitiveness when everything in the world is achieved only by competing? I feel that even when I try my hardest, I'm unable to keep up with the pace of those who are racing past me."

"It's easy! You don't have to keep up with anyone else's pace," said Shambhu, shaking his head. "You have to set your own pace, and then stay confident with it. You don't have to feel threatened if someone else does well too. Just stay calm and be still—unprovoked and unruffled."

Aditya looked hopeless, "That's not easy."

Shambhu gazed at him patiently, "The problem is that all you know is to run thoughtlessly—sometimes even in circles. You don't know how to be still. You must strike a balance between movement and stillness. How can you receive anything from the universe if you're constantly in a chaotic state?"

Aditya was unable to understand this advice, "No Shambhu! It's impossible to sit still when I constantly feel the need to be doing more, and then some more!"

Shambhu looked at him with compassion in his eyes, "You don't have to do more, Aditya. You have done enough. You just need to trust the universe more. Tell me, have you seen the mountains?"

Aditya watched as Shambhu stood up, raising his hands.

Shambhu questioned Aditya, "Why do you think the mountains stand proudly rooted to a spot, confident in their identities? Why don't they rush around and compare themselves to each other?"

A peacock was singing behind a cluster of trees nearby.

"Aditya, this is the second law of happiness—to receive from the cosmos, you must first work as hard as you can and then stay confident and calm. I know that maintaining composure always is difficult! On a bad day, some events will set you off and you'll want to break down in a bundle of chaos. It would require all your courage and determination to find peace, especially when you feel that the whole world around you is conspiring against you."

"What is chaos?" Aditya questioned, as he felt a familiar darkness seeping into his spirit at the memory of the turmoil that he had been through recently.

"Dark and depressing thoughts arise when you compare yourself with others, when your need to surpass others overpowers you, causing your anxiety to take charge and trick you into thinking that you are losing to others in this mythical race. All this, my friend, is called chaos."

Every word hit Aditya like a stone thrown into a pool of loneliness in which he had been hiding himself for years.

"Will I receive happiness if I stay calm?" he asked.

"Your efforts can't go unrewarded. That's the law of this universe. They will come back and find you. However, please quit comparing! Everyone's journey is different."

Shambhu was standing in the middle of a circular patch of grass with his feet firmly placed on the ground, as though they had taken strong roots in the ground. His shoulders were wide apart. He was looking straight in front of himself.

Aditya stood in front of Shambhu, breathing evenly, in sync with him.

"Aditya, this is *Tadasana*, the mountain pose. Stand still, and be fully aware of the here and now! Be mindful and trusting of the universe around you. You have done enough. Now allow yourself to feel calm, and powerful. What is supposed to come to you, will come. It will find its way, now more easily than before because you are standing calmly to receive it."

Aditya stood there, his eyes closed, rooted to a point of the earth, listening to Shambhu's words.

"What is supposed to be yours, will come to you. No one can take it away...."

What was this beautiful, unfamiliar emotion that he was feeling? he wondered.

For so many days, he had been chasing a speeding clock. No matter how fast he ran, the clock always seemed to run faster. The minutes and seconds rushed past him, jeering at him, as he limped behind time.

Always behind schedule, always behind deadlines, Aditya was acutely aware of the dreadful screeching sound time made as it whizzed past his ears.

Now it seemed as if time had decided to become his companion. It had slowed down. It was not competing with him anymore. It was now keeping pace with him, following every breath of his.

"Open your eyes slowly, Aditya," Shambhu said gently.

Aditya obeyed him, opening his eyes as slowly as he could, letting the soothing sight of the green grass seep into his consciousness.

"Shambhu, that was amazing," Aditya exclaimed excitedly.

"Ssshhhh…" Shambhu put a finger on Aditya's lips. Silence flowed between the two friends like a gently gurgling, peaceful river.

Date: FEBRUARY 24, 2029 | Time: 1:10 PM

The Eagle Arrives

When was the last time Aditya had felt this peaceful? He just could not remember it.

He was sitting on the grass, watching a butterfly that was coloured in vibrant hues, flitting over red and yellow roses. Bholu was running around in circles as always, chasing the butterfly and barking happily.

After a while, he looked around, wondering where Shambhu was.

He looked back towards the butterfly, but it had flown away. All of a sudden, he heard a strange noise which seemed to echo loudly in the garden.

Where was the noise coming from?

"Shambhu! Shambhu! Shambhu!" He started shouting as he took off running in the direction of the sound.

The garden echoed with his voice, but no one answered.

Aditya felt a fresh wave of anxiety running through his body.

Had he lost his friend?

In just a couple of hours both of them had developed a strong bond. He could not bear it if his new friend suddenly disappeared. He felt the familiar anxiety descending on him, like a dark black cloud advancing upon him.

As he ran around the trees, he abruptly came to a stop.

There behind the giant tree, in a clearing where white *shiuli* flowers were falling from the tree, Shambhu was sitting calmly. But there was something else. Shambhu was not alone.

As Aditya inched closer, he saw a large eagle perched on Shambhu's shoulder. The eagle was looking down at Shambhu, its beak near his nose. Strangely, both Shambhu and the eagle seemed to be communicating in a secret, silent language.

All of a sudden, the eagle raised and fluttered its enormous wings.

Terrified, Aditya screamed loudly. In his attempt to save Shambhu from the eagle, he dashed towards him with his hands raised, trying to shoo the eagle away.

Hearing his screams, Shambhu turned to look at Aditya. First he looked surprised, and in the next moment he burst into laughter.

Aditya stopped short, looking perplexed. Why does

Shambhu laugh so much? And when he laughs, he really laughs with his entire body, heart and soul!

In response to his screams, the eagle hopped to one side. It now sat on the grass and looked at Aditya with its huge, penetrating eyes.

Aditya stood at a distance uncertainly and asked, "Shambhu, why do you laugh so much?"

Shambhu doubled with laughter and took his own sweet time to answer his question. Aditya was left with no choice but to stand and wait.

Shambhu sat up and looked at him, "Aditya, my dear, why don't you laugh more? And tell me, are you afraid of eagles too?"

Aditya felt defensive and irritated. "I have never seen an eagle so closely. Don't they fly far above in the sky?"

Shambhu turned to face the eagle. It was sitting across from both of them, looking at them with a detached air. Instead of answering Aditya, he shifted the topic of discussion.

"Aditya, remember you told me that you had the worst day of your life. I assume, a crisis took place today?"

Aditya looked crestfallen. "I got suspended from my school today. It started this way.... I had an argument with my favourite teacher. He lost his temper and dragged me to the principal's office. I tried to tell the principal my point of view, but he refused to hear me out. Then he suspended me and called my mother. I did not feel like going home and facing everyone, so I decided to spend some time in this garden."

Shambhu was listening to him, his eyes twinkling with amusement. "Tell me more about it."

When No One Chose Me

Once again, it had happened. Once again, there was no reason why it should have happened.

Just a week ago, it was announced in school that there would be a day trip to half a dozen famous monuments in the city. Despite my ongoing depression, I was thrilled! I have always been fascinated with history. Ever since the announcement was made, I began researching every destination that we would visit.

I could talk of nothing else with my brothers, Pankaj and Prakhar. I told Mummy to pack my favourite snacks for the day excursions. My family was overjoyed to see me happy once again.

And today, just a day before the trip, everything got spoilt.

Amit Sir announced that all the boys attending the day trip will have to walk with a partner in order to ensure their safety and reduce the risk of getting lost during the day. The best thing was that the boys could choose their own partners. Amit Sir instructed them to begin naming their selected mates so that he could write the names of all the pairs down.

I felt a small nagging doubt in the pit of my stomach. I was sure that no one was going to pick me.

Though my parents and brothers didn't know this, the truth is that I was far from being a popular boy. I don't belong to any group of boys. I like studying by myself most of the time, and I even have lunch by myself during breaks. Not surprisingly, I am called a loner by everyone. I am aware that most boys make fun of me behind my back, and at some painful moments, directly in front of me.

That is why I was worried sick just now. What happens if no one chooses me as their partner? It would be mortifying! It would be humiliating, literally.

I made an effort to convince myself that it couldn't be possible that I would be without a partner. By the law of mathematics, there are forty boys in the classroom, so I had to have a partner. Somebody will definitely choose me.

Yet, that feeling would not go away. I started feeling increasingly uneasy and nervous.

Sir started calling out the names of the boys in the order of the way they sat in the class. I sat at the back of the class, so my name would be called out last. Siddharth sat next to me and we never talked to each other. In response to Sir, the student whose name was being called out would reply with the name of the chosen partner. The most popular boys were being fought for. Laughter and jokes echoed in the air. The boys who found their favourite mates were shaking hands with obvious camaraderie.

As the list progressed, I started praying that at least someone would take my name. But then, my worst fear came true. By the time the list came to end I realised that not a single person had taken my name.

No one!

I tried to fight the growing panic that was threatening to overwhelm me. Finally only two names were left... Siddharth's and mine. Siddharth was being asked first. He took the names of two other boys, but he was told that his choices had already found their partners and that could not be changed. In response, Siddharth stood there silently and sulkily. Amit Sir looked at him and spoke, "Siddharth, it's just you and Aditya now. So you have to go together."

Siddharth looked devastated, "No Sir... Not Aditya!"

That was not necessary, Siddharth. That was like rubbing salt on my wounds.

I could see that even Amit Sir did not like his attitude.

He shook his head firmly and shut his register with a final thump, "You have no choice, Siddharth. It's you and Aditya!"

At that moment, Amit Sir gave me a sad, rather empathetic look. I could hear a few boys chuckling to themselves, trying to hide their smiles. I was sure that they were mocking me.

Siddhartha shrugged and spoke no more.

I was stung with humiliation and rage. I started feeling a familiar anger rising inside me. The next moment I was on my feet, "It's alright, Sir. If Siddharth doesn't want to be with me, please don't force him. I want to be alone. I don't need anyone."

Amit Sir looked surprised for an instant. Then he said firmly, "That's not something that you get to decide, Aditya. Rules are rules, and everyone must follow them."

I flared up immediately, "Why can't I decide what I want to do? Isn't it my life? Why should I be always burdened with decisions made by others? I don't want to be with someone who doesn't want to be my partner. That's it ! How can you force me?"

The next thing I knew, Amit Sir lost his temper, "Don't you dare argue with me. What has happened to you, Aditya? You were the most pleasant and easy-going boy in this class. Now you're the most difficult child in this class."

That was it!

A raging fury exploded inside me. All my emotions which had been pent up for months suddenly erupted into a volcano in one second.

I don't remember the sequence of events clearly following my explosion. All I can recollect is that I threw my bag on the floor angrily. My books, pencil box and geometry set clattered onto the floor. A collective, sharp gasp made by all the students at this unexpected defiance echoed in the silent classroom.

Amit Sir's face was red with anger. He could hardly believe the shocking display of disobedience that had happened in his class.

"C'mon, young man! We're marching to the Principal's office."

Date: FEBRUARY 24, 2029 | Time: 2.05 PM

Rise Like An Eagle

Aditya stopped speaking.

He glanced at Shambhu, who was sitting next to him, listening silently.

Thankfully, Shambhu did not laugh this time. Instead he nodded and patted Aditya's hand, "So I understand that Amit Sir spoke to you angrily, and you reacted immediately."

Aditya's face was red with pent up emotions, "Yes, I felt humiliated, and I retorted back, which made him even angrier."

Shambhu looked straight in his eyes, "Why did you retort back? By the tone of his voice, you must have understood that there was a storm brewing....Why did you feel the need to dive right in?"

Aditya shrugged angrily, "It's only natural that I would react, isn't it? I am a loner, that's what everyone says! I hate that tag! I detest having this rubbed in my face constantly."

"Calm down, Aditya. Breathe, the way I taught you," Shambhu spoke firmly, and yet gently. Though unwillingly, Aditya breathed in and out and felt himself getting calmer right away.

Shambhu was sitting back against a large tree, "Retorting back aggressively in response to an angry person just makes everything worse. Amit Sir's anger was like a violent storm and you just charged blindly, straight into it Sometimes, a storm may appear to be easy to handle outwardly, but in reality it may be brewing with unseen forces that could overpower you any moment. "

Aditya replied, "So what else can I do? If I can't muster the guts to fight the storm, then I'll lose all the self-respect I have. Should I just cower and hide?"

In response, Shambhu smiled, "Aditya, let me tell you something about eagles."

Bholu was sleeping soundly on the grass.

Shambhu continued, "Do you know what happens to birds when a storm starts? Most birds get frightened and hide in their shelters, waiting for the fury of the storm to pass. Yet, some other reckless birds rush into the storm, because they want to keep flying!"

Aditya waited for Shambhu to speak further. Shambhu was looking upwards, his eyes lost in the unseen heights of the vast expanse of the blue sky. "Aditya, unlike both of those fearful or angry birds, the mighty eagle neither hides from the storm, nor does it try to fly in it. Instead, the eagle keeps calm and instinctively determines the strength of the storm. Then accordingly it propels itself upwards using the suction created by the storm. It rises high, and keeps rising higher until it's flying far above the sucking funnel of the storm, where it is safe and sound. And there, it flies in peace, looking down at the storm, and the eternity."

Aditya's eyes became large with astonishment as he looked at the eagle sitting in front of them.

Shambhu spoke, "Aditya, do you understand what I am saying? Today you behaved like those foolhardy birds who rush into the storm without thinking. What you needed to do was to stay calm, because all storms eventually run out of rain. You needed to keep your emotions in control. Remember two things—first, storms don't last; and second, their strength can be used to rise up in life."

Aditya was quiet, thinking hard. He looked at the eagle again. It was now calmly drinking water from a sprinkler that was splashing all over the green grass.

After some moments of profound silence, he spoke, "I also wish to be powerful and mighty like the eagle, Shambhu."

Shambhu cupped his hand and filled water in it. The eagle hopped over to him and started drinking water right from his hand. Aditya once again marveled at the silent camaraderie Shambhu had with all animals and birds.

"Aditya, you must remember that at least four times in their lifetime, eagles go through a painful process of molting. They shed their old feathers, one by one. Then, they sit there and wait patiently for the new wings to appear. It takes time, one painful moment after another. All that while, they do not panic. They know that this is the rule of nature—to let go of the old, and embrace the new. Eagles don't cry over old feathers shedding off, and floating into nothingness. They accept it. They know that their new feathers will give them renewed strength and power. They have faith, and they don't question it."

"Do they sit alone during that painful experience, or do they have others with them?" Aditya asked hopefully.

Shambhu looked into Aditya's eyes and smiled. "Aditya, eagles usually stay alone. They prefer a solitary existence. They fly alone, traversing the quiet silences in the high sky. Imagine if they constantly sought the company of others, always in a group, screeching and fighting over grains of food. Surely, they wouldn't be able to scale heights of the limitless skies."

Aditya confessed, "I like to stay alone too, especially when I am working or reading. People say that I'm a freak. Sometimes they call me an introvert, and sometimes they call me a loser. Some of them even question my mental health."

Shambhu put an arm around him comfortingly,

"If you need to paint a beautiful painting, or write a meaningful book, or study something; then surely you need to be alone for long periods of time. None of this can be done while trying to please or planning your day to accommodate other people's plans. If you want to achieve anything big or powerful in life, Aditya, become an eagle!"

Aditya looked up at him with his eyes shining.

"Yes Aditya! This is the third law of happiness. Fly like an eagle! Rise like an eagle!"

"Yes!" Aditya whispered under his breath.

"C'mon, Aditya! Let's try to imitate the eagle!" Shambhu shouted already running towards a tree...

Aditya ran after him, their joyful shouts reverberating in the trees around them.

Beneath the tree, Shambhu was standing straight, contorting his limbs.

"Now what's this? I thought we were going to fly!" Aditya laughed.

"Just follow me!" Shambhu urged.

Aditya looked at him, and then just like him, bent his knees, crossing one of his legs and arms over the other one. He placed his palms in front of his chest. In an instant, he realised that this pose resembled the beak of an eagle.

Despite his best efforts, he lost his balance a few times and lurched to his side. Yet, he did not give up. He was determined to follow the example of the eagle, which had inspired him so much.

All of a sudden, he realised that he was standing straight and was not falling!

"Look Shambhu! Look at me!" Aditya said happily.

'You're doing the *Garudasan*, Aditya," Shambhu answered.

The two boys stood side by side, maintaining their balance. Bholu jumped around both of them, playing happily.

The eagle sitting nearby had drunk water and rested. It was now ready to fly. It opened its large, mighty wings, and took off in the faraway skies, its eyes searching for distant stars and unknown galaxies.

Date: FEBRUARY 24, 2029 | Time: 2.35 PM

Shadows Under The Eyes

The sun was at the zenith of the sky, bathing everything in a magnificent, golden light. The leaves on the green trees seemed to light up in an ethereal, luminescent manner, glowing like molten, liquid gold.

The boys had just sat down on the grass with Bholu to rest, when Aditya noticed that Shambhu was looking at his face intently.

"What happened now, Shambhu? Why are you looking at me this way?" Aditya asked, feeling uneasy.

"Tell me, why do you have dark circles under your eyes?" Shambhu's gaze was intense.

Aditya felt embarrassed and rubbed his eyes, "That's because I haven't slept properly for many days. I sleep for a couple of hours and then wake up with a start. I think I am suffering from anxiety."

"Tell me more about this," Shambhu sat down on the grass, pulling out some oranges from his bag.

The boys sat together, peeling juicy oranges and eating them hungrily. Aditya had never been fond of fruits, but today the oranges tasted heavenly. He realised that everything seemed wonderful with Shambhu, even eating oranges!

Aditya tried to remember when the long, sleepless nights had started. He was lost in his memories when he realised that Shambhu was climbing a rather gigantic tree.

Why can't Shambhu be still for even a moment!

"Hey Shambhu!" Aditya called out to his friend who was hardly visible through the dense foliage of the tree.

"I can hear you! Tell me about your sleepless nights!" Shambhu shouted back.

When My Sleep Said Goodbye

Everyone's life had gone through a major transformation since Covid started a decade back. However, the lives of the students had changed the most.

Before Covid, children would run in playgrounds, and jostle each other about in school buses. They would be out early in the morning, and return to their homes in the evening after attending their schools and tuitions. They were going through the most idyllic period of their lives—their childhood and adolescence.

Covid lockdowns changed everything. All of a sudden, they were confined to their houses. Away from their friends and classmates, they had to learn to study through online classes. Their movements were restricted and their minds fogged up.

Their dependence on the internet escalated every day, till a point came that the moment they opened their eyes, they would reach out for their laptops and phones. The last thing they looked at before they slept was the screens of their devices. In fact, their entire universe was limited to the screens of their phones.

The internet dominated every aspect of their lives, including their knowledge, learning, examinations, relationships and entertainment.

Like many others, I was a bit reluctant to use the internet at first. I had always been an active, agile boy. I hated to be confined to one spot for a long time, and I would get restless. But now, I had no choice.

There was nowhere I could go, and no one that I could play with. Without relying on the internet, I couldn't even get new books to read, music to listen to, or movies to watch.

Slowly, and without even realising, I became an expert at juggling my online classes and tuitions, watching movies and connecting with my friends online.

Habits are not easy to forget and so, even when the lockdown was over, my routine remained the same. Most of the times, I would comfortably lie in my bed, my phone by my side and my laptop open in front of me with a steaming hot cup of coffee near me. At that moment, I would feel all powerful, the entire universe at the flick of my fingertips.

Initially it was just work that I focused on. But slowly, I started spending time on social media platforms. I would scroll through the media accounts of my friends and cousins, my mind caught in an endless loop of curiosity and judgement.

That was also the time when I fell in love for the first time. I had joined a special coaching class where only the most brilliant students were chosen through a national level entrance test. Aditi happened to be in my coaching class, also aspiring to be a doctor.

It started when she asked me to lend her my physics notes. Over the next few months, we became good friends over many discussions of Physics laws and Math calculations. I would spend hours explaining complicated theorems to Aditi, lost in her eyes.

Life had never been more beautiful. I couldn't wait to get up in the morning and rush to the coaching class after school. A couple of boys who had noticed the change in my behaviour started teasing and nudging me every time Aditi would pass by. I started basking under this sudden attention and camaraderie. Soon enough, they started pushing me to ask her out for a date. It took me several days to gather courage, and one day everything just fell into place.

On one summer afternoon, the results of a weekly test were announced. I was thrilled to know that I had topped in the class. Everyone including Aditi congratulated me. My new found success gave me confidence enough to shyly ask her out for coffee.

When she agreed, I felt that this had to be the happiest day of my life. What more could a boy ask for? I was doing so well in my studies and going out with the girl of my dreams.

I started dreaming of a rosy future, adorned with the fulfilment of all my dreams.

But the promised future did not come.

Aditi contacted me the following day and abruptly cancelled our date, giving me an excuse. Despite my extreme disappointment, I made an effort to maintain my optimism.

It got worse over the course of the next few days. Aditi began to distance herself from me. Also, she started hanging out with a popular and a rather loud set of students. It was obvious that she had told them about my embarrassing effort to ask her out. Whenever I would pass by, they would start laughing and calling out Aditi's name, jeering and doubling with mirth. She would just stand there, laughing with them.

I did not know which was worse, her crushing rejection or the onslaught of bullying that I was facing. I withdrew into a shell, keeping to myself and not communicating with anyone. I seethed with impotent rage and suffered with depression. With nothing better to do, I began to spend time on the internet, checking the activities of Aditi and her friends online.

I did not even realise when I started spending hours looking at the rosy, illusionary pictures of their lives. With time, my mind became an insatiable beast that was constantly consuming posts, pictures, tags and captions. The smiling faces of the people whom I was nearly stalking got imprinted on my mind, constantly reminding me that I am a loser.

I looked at those glowing, beaming pictures shimmering on the screen, and then looked around myself.

What was I? A boy sitting alone, in an ordinary room. Friendless! Lonely! No one cared for me! No one wanted me! I was doomed to a solitary, forgotten existence forever.

The sleepless nights started then.

I just couldn't sleep as I would wake up at nights, looking at those pictures again and again.

What was I hoping for? That these pictures jeering at me would change magically?

But pictures do not change. They remain still, absolutely frozen. No matter what time of the day or night I looked at them, they stayed the same. The same smiling faces, the same bright colors!

Yet, with every view, they enforced the loneliness inside me, digging a hole so deep in my soul that I felt that I could never be whole again.

Yes, that was probably the time when those sleepless nights started.

Date: FEBRUARY 24, 2029 | Time: 3.10 PM

Rest Like A Child

Aditya wiped the tears that were about to roll down his cheeks with his sleeves and tried to smile. This was the first time that he had confided in another person about the most painful incident of his life.

Shambhu broke the silence from the tree top above, his voice booming "Is that it? Nothing more?"

Aditya shook his head. "I don't have anything to say anymore. You say something!"

Shambhu shouted from the treetop, "My stupid friend, why do you like to tell yourself untrue horror stories?"

Aditya was confused, "Which horror stories?"

Shambhu's voice boomed through the leaves again, "Horror stories like… 'Oh, others are so popular and happy, while I am struggling with loneliness.' Not one of these presumptions is true. You have a distorted view of your own life, and also of others. You are focused on the lens of social media, which is nothing but an illusion."

Aditya looked pensive, "But those pictures? Are those pictures a lie too?"

Shambhu laughed loudly, "The pictures are real, but remember, those pictures are carefully chosen by people to project a certain reality. Everybody wants to project a rosy picture of happiness and prosperity, and that alone. Whose life can be just yang, and not yin?"

"What's yin and yang?" Aditya looked puzzled.

Shambhu's face was now peering at him through the leaves, "That's the principle of the universe. Yin is dark, and yang is light. They both co-exist, and are complementary forces. The perfectly curated pictures that you see on social media defy that principle. They project a person's life as all light, with no darkness. They also create an imbalance in the mind of the person who is viewing them, and believing their narrative."

"A person… like me?" Aditya asked.

"Yes. Your perception about those pictures is misleading, but you don't even know it, and you never question it. You believe it blindly. And then you tell yourself scary stories."

Aditya wiped a tear, "I wish I could be confident in my own space, and not need others to love me."

Shambhu laughed, "There is no harm in wanting others to love you. However, do remember that you're most vulnerable when you want someone to love you back. Your vulnerability shifts your confidence from your hands to that person. You start looking at yourself from that person's eyes. If that person shows disinterest, you tell yourself that you're worthless. If that person seems to prefer someone else to you, then you fall into a self-destructive cycle of self-loathing. It digs a hole inside you, and your self-confidence slips away. Aditya, your worth is not dependent on anyone's interest in you. Make your own relationship with yourself so strong that no one can shatter your own image in your eyes. Cheer for yourself. Pat yourself on your back. You're a fine, exquisite and wonderful piece of work. Love yourself. Aditya!"

"Easier said than done, my friend!" Aditya retorted.

Shambhu shouted back, "It would be easier if you let it happen, instead of being obsessed about it. You subject yourself to sitting in a room alone, staring at your fears that are like a snake in front of you. You keep sitting like a paralysed person in front of this snake, day and night, sometimes frozen at one spot, telling yourself frightening things."

Aditya was listening, his eyes brimming with sadness, "I don't want to be this person who is rooted to one spot looking at this snake which won't go away, no matter how much I strike it!"

Shambhu was ready with an answer, "Of course the snake won't go away! That's simply because the snake does not exist!"

Aditya was surprised. "If it does not exist, why am I seeing it?"

Shambhu was sitting comfortably on the highest branch of the tree, sniffing a white flower, "That's your mind playing tricks on you. You have not guarded your mind, and so your mind is running wild. It sees a rope and thinks that it is a snake. It sees a rock and imagines that it is a bull charging at you. Those are just your fears which have been left unattended without control."

Aditya climbed the first branch of the tree, craned his neck and looked up at Shambhu, "Why would my fears do that?"

Shambhu shouted back, "As long as you are the captain of your ship, and fears are just your workers who guide you through a stormy sea, it's all good. But Aditya, what happens when you get overwhelmed with panic and anxiety and lose your grip on the steering wheel of your ship? Then fears displace you from the captain's seat and start steering the ship of your life. The problem is that your fears which are actually steering your ship don't have a good eyesight. They were never meant to be captains of any ship. They have a blind, heightened sense of danger, an intuition that goes haywire when left uncontrolled. They sense danger everywhere; they imagine things which do not exist. They come to wrong conclusions and they think that they are always right!"

"And they are not always right?" Aditya asked slowly.

"No Aditya! Your fears might mistake a gentle wave to be tsunami and press the panic button. You would end up focusing on a rather unimportant event or detail. In that process, you would not have the courage to take your ship out in the seas."

"What should I do then?" Aditya asked worriedly.

"Take over your ship, Aditya. Tell your fears to leave immediately. Tell them that their time is up. Have faith in yourself. You are a skilled captain. Don't forget your own powers. Take a deep breath, and start again."

"And what about those people jeering at me? Bullying me?" Aditya looked hurt.

"Ignore those people. Remember the eagle and the storm! You are the eagle, and they are the storm. You can't reach your destination if you keep stopping on your way to grapple with every storm. Choose your battles wisely. People who stand in a crowd and laugh at others don't deserve your attention. Ignore them and fly high."

Aditya stood quietly, absorbing every word, feeling his confidence returning to him, like blood which starts flowing in the veins again.

"Aditya, first, leave your phone alone!" Shambhu spoke.

Aditya glanced at his phone. He realised that the phone was discharged. He frowned as he wondered how that had happened. He had charged his phone fully just hours ago.

Shambhu was impatient, "Leave it alone!"

Aditya kept the discharged phone on the nearby bench and walked towards Shambhu, “Ok Sir!” he laughed.

Shambhu looked satisfied, “Do you remember the time when you were a child, say about five years old?”

Aditya remembered those days very well. It was the time before the Covid Pandemic had arrived. That had been the happiest period of his life. He had been a naughty and mischievous child, bright eyed and full of energy. His life was beyond any care. His days were busy, full of games and fun with his friends. He would eat his dinner sleepily, so exhausted he would be! Finally, he would fall asleep as soon as his head hit the pillow.

Now he looked at Shambhu and tried to smile somehow. He felt that Shambhu could read his mind completely. He did not even have to say anything.

Shambhu was smiling back, “Aditya, let me take you back to your childhood. Come on! Let’s kneel on the ground.”

Aditya shook his head and laughed. Shambhu and his tricks!

He kneeled by Shambhu’s side and smiled at him, “And now what?”

“Remember how you used to flop on the ground when you were a child? Let’s do that! Bend forwards, stretching your hands!”

Aditya laughed again, following his friend’s movements.

Shambhu was stretching, with his fingers pointing in front, his forehead touching the ground.

Aditya forced his tense, rigid muscles to follow Shambhu. First one, then second, then third.... He started feeling every muscle of his body relaxing slowly, and surely.

He closed his eyes and imagined himself sinking into a soft cloud of comfort which enveloped him completely. The cloud was caressing him with its feathery, cool arms, stroking his forehead with a soothing touch. He was floating in the cloud now, entering into a peaceful universe that nurtured and calmed him.

He heard Shambhu's voice at a distance, "This is the fourth rule of happiness—to rest like a child. You're doing the *Bal asana*, the child's pose."

Aditya could not answer. He had not slept for many days. Now he felt his eyes getting heavy and closing on their own.

Aditya slept.

Date: FEBRUARY 24, 2020 | Time: 4.00 PM

Playing In The Past

Aditya lay on the grass, sleeping in a deep slumber. It was as if he was compensating for all the countless nights that he had not been able to sleep in the past.

The sun had moved its onward journey in the day. It was no longer at the top of the sky. It had moved westwards and downwards as though it was following the axis of an invisible wheel.

Shambhu had left some time ago to get sandwiches for both of them. Aditya had not eaten anything since morning. His packed lunch box had been in his bag, which he had left in the car.

Aditya was startled awake by a thundering sound. He sat up and looked from side to side, alarmed. Now what was that?

Soon enough he saw the source of that sound. It was Shambhu!

Shambhu was sprinting with a stick in his hand,

nudging a tyre of a car which was revolving merrily in front of him. In the other hand, he clutched a paper envelope which Aditya hoped carried their sandwiches,

"Oh God! It's you, Shambhu!" Aditya let out a cry.

Shambhu gave the tyre one last shove and it flopped on the grass in abandon. His face was glowing red with all the running and his happiness knew no bounds. He sat on the grass and opened the paper bag.

"C'mon Aditya, let's eat!" He started laying the sandwiches on the paper plates that he had brought along.

"I've never seen a more playful boy than you." Aditya shook his head, taking a bite of the sandwich eagerly.

Emerging from behind a bush, Bholu joined them in devouring the sandwiches.

With a smile, Shambhu asked, "So what would you gain by not being playful? You should enjoy every moment of your life. This life has been given to you to play, and laugh!"

"I used to play a lot when I was a child. I was the football captain of my school team. But then, back in those days, I didn't have the pressure of studies. Not anymore...," Aditya spoke guardedly.

"Huh! Why not anymore?" Shambhu spoke indistinctly, through a mouthful of the sandwich.

"Playing is for children, who are free, with no responsibilities." Aditya countered.

Shambhu looked surprised, "Why should playing be for only children? Playing is for everyone, no matter what your age is!"

Aditya did not feel like speaking more on this subject. It hurt him too much. He felt those familiar tears threatening to fill his eyes again.

Shambhu smiled understandingly, "Now c'mon! Tell me."

Flying Free Like The Wind

Back in those days, I would wake up at the crack of the dawn at 4.30 AM every day. It would still be dark at that time of the morning. The moment my eyes would open, I would swiftly turn the alarm off, so that my sleeping brothers would not wake up.

Then, I would roll out of bed and start getting ready as quietly as possible. The sound of the flowing water in the bathroom would be muted. The opening and closing of doors would be hardly heard by anyone. I used to make sure that all my clothes and shoes were already laid out the night before so that I didn't have to search for them in the morning. My T-shirt and shorts would be ready, waiting for me, on a chair.

Everything was perfect. Everything was synchronised.

Once I was dressed, I would make my way into the kitchen to warm up a glass of sugary milk. The scent of the comforting, warm milk would fill the morning air, as

I would drink it slowly, feeling a fresh, pulsating vitality coursing through my body.

Next, I would walk out of the home stealthily while everyone was still sleeping. I would click the door lock and then walk towards my bicycle in the front yard.

I would stop there for a moment to breathe in the early fragrant morning air filling up my lungs.

At that moment of time, I would be captivated by the miracle of life. Overwhelmed, I would close my eyes and listen to the birds chirping in the green trees.

What a beautiful day it was!

Then I would start pedalling the bicycle as fast as I could, racing on the empty roads. My hair would be flying in the breeze as I would gaze at the road which would take me straight to the place where my heart lay… the football ground.

As I approached the ground, my eyes would look for the vast expanse of the green field as it got visible. Surely this was heaven!

As I would reach even closer, my eyes would search for my friends waiting for me. The moment they would see me, a loud cheer would fill the morning sky. I would park my bicycle in a hurry and go sprinting towards them, shouting greetings, teasing them and challenging them.

Soon enough, the match would start with a sharp whistle piercing the morning air. The thudding sound of the ball against their shoes, the boyish youthful shouts as the game progressed, the sudden goals and the loud cheers… I felt close to God in those moments.

Now it's all a memory. For the last three years, I have not stepped on a football ground. My parents and teachers had advised me to quit playing sports as I had to concentrate on my board examination and entrance exams for a reputed university. I had agreed reluctantly.

It seemed like a very practical and sensible decision.

Yet, I know that my happiness is gone… all gone.

Date: FEBRUARY 24, 2029 | Time: 5.00 PM

Dance Like A River

Aditya was sitting with a sandwich in his hand, staring at a distance. Bholu was sleeping after eating the sandwiches.

All of a sudden, he felt drops of water falling on his head. Looking up, he saw that the sun in the sky had begun to set in the western sky. Dark, heavy clouds were billowing in the cool wind.

"Shambhu, look! It's about to rain!"

Glancing up at the sky, Shambhu smiled happily. Velvety raindrops started falling on their heads, caressing their eyelids and cheeks. At a distance, peacocks started to call out joyfully. Koels were beckoning the harbingers of happiness in unison. It seemed as if the entire universe was dancing along in a cosmic celebration.

Aditya covered his head with his hands and looked around for cover. Thankfully there was a shaded canopy nearby.

"Shambhu, move quickly! Come along!" he shouted.

To his surprise, Shambhu rose to his feet, looked skyward, closed his eyes and opened his arms.

"Shambhu, it's raining harder! What are you doing?" Aditya cried out. He tried to grab Shambhu's hand in an attempt to pull his friend to safety.

"Let go of me!" said Shambhu, pushing Aditya away.

Aditya was puzzled. What was wrong with his friend? He was usually so amiable and easy going. He had never seen him getting this disagreeable.

"Shambhu, you'll get wet in the rain," Aditya piped up, uncertainly.

Shambhu did not reply. He was whirling at one spot, with his eyes closed, his arms outstretched, lost in his own world. He had a happy smile on his face. He looked like he had suddenly been blessed with wings. Bholu woke up and joined Shambhu, hopping and dancing around him.

Aditya stood under the shade, unsure what to do next.

Shambhu opened his eyes and looked at Aditya. His eyes were twinkling with excitement. "Let's play football, Aditya! In the rain! That big tree out there will be our goalpost!"

Aditya was trying to shield his face from the onslaught of raindrops. He shouted, "It's the time to save yourself from rain! And where will you get a football in this isolated garden?"

Shambhu laughed, "Why must you try to save yourself from this beautiful rain? The earth is dancing. You must dance with it too! And look, here is a football!"

Aditya looked in surprise as Shambhu fetched a football from behind a bush.

Aditya remembered how he used to play in the rain with his friends years ago. Through the long, winding tunnel of time, he could still hear the joyful shouting and yelling, echoing in his ears now.

But that was so long ago! he thought.

Since years, whenever it rained, his first instinct was to run for cover. He would carry his umbrella and raincoat with him whenever he stepped out. The moment the first raindrops fell, his umbrella would be unfurled to protect him. Just to be sure that not even a single raindrop could touch him, he would wear his raincoat which covered even his ankles and hands.

And now Shambhu was asking him to play football in this pouring rain!

Yet, how could he say no to his friend? He stepped out of his shelter and stood uncertainly near Shambhu.

Does he even remember how to play? It had been ages ago. He looked unsure, as he started nudging the ball with his feet hesitantly.

To his amazement, Shambhu turned out to be a surprisingly nimble player. Without giving him a moment to react, Shambhu tackled the ball expertly from him. Aditya stood there, stunned at the expertise of his friend.

Something that had been buried deep inside him started stirring. A familiar energy was washing over his sleeping spirit. His leg lifted up on its own, and his muscles arched up.

The next moment, Aditya threw himself in the game. He was suddenly off and running. He tackled the ball back from Shambhu, as the earth started spinning around him, at a pace which seemed to accelerate every moment. An unfamiliar vitality was pumping in his veins, as he ran and jumped, kicked and hit the ball.

"Goal!!" Aditya shouted with happiness as he kicked the ball right at the big tree, "I am playing! See Shambhu, I am playing!"

Shambhu laughed, "You are actually meditating, my dear Aditya."

Aditya stopped playing and stood still, "Is this meditation?"

Shambhu nodded, as raindrops flowed down his cheeks, "Yes Aditya! You are moving, like the earth moves around its axis around the sun, the way all planets move. You're not just playing; you're actually releasing your spiritual energy from your soul. You're actually meditating, in full control of your body and mind. C'mon, don't just stand there. Get moving again!"

Aditya laughed and the game resumed.

The two boys played an energetic game over the course of the next half an hour, as gentle rain poured down at them. Bholu ran around with them, barking happily.

At the end of the game, Aditya fell on the ground, feeling overwhelmed. He was taken by surprise by the sudden, unexpected tears in his eyes which flowed down his cheeks along with the raindrops. He felt a giant emotion exploding inside him and soon, he was sobbing his heart out.

Shambhu sat next to him and put an arm around him comfortingly. "Why am I crying, Shambhu?" Aditya asked as his body was wracked in sobs.

Shambhu replied, "It's good to cry. Just let it all out. Why do you keep your emotions bottled up?"

It had been so long that Aditya had felt anything. He had been completely numb since months. He had been so terrified of facing his feelings that he had developed the habit of burying them deep inside.

And now this flood of emotions!

"Tell me, what are you feeling, Aditya?" Shambhu was gripping his hand.

"For many days, I have been feeling so low. I feel as if everything is finished! Everything has gone wrong, Shambhu! Everything which was in its place some years ago has collapsed now." Aditya sobbed.

Shambhu smiled, "Everything was in its place some years back, I agree. But even now, everything is in its place. Everything was right then and everything is right now."

Aditya looked at him in surprise, "What are you saying, Shambhu? You don't know how my life has derailed. You don't know how my dreams have broken. You have no idea how lonely I am."

Shambhu nodded, "I know everything, Aditya. But tell me why do you know that your life has been derailed?"

Aditya shrugged, "... Because I tried everything. I gave up my favorite hobbies. I gave up my sleep and rest. And yet, nothing has worked according to my plans, or my parents' plans."

Shambhu smiled with a twinkle in his eyes and completed his sentence, "Or your teacher's plans, or your brother's plans, right?"

"Those too...," Aditya nodded.

"And what about God's plans?" Shambhu asked.

Aditya looked puzzled, "How would I know what His plans are? I can't see Him. I can't talk to Him."

Shambhu laughed, "Oh Aditya! You can! He is always around you. Just like the air you breathe... and of course, you know what His plans are. These plans that are unfolding in front of you.... don't you understand that these are God's plans!"

Aditya looked at Shambhu in surprise, "Why would God have such terrible plans for me? Why would He make me suffer so much? Surely He can't be so cruel!

I have been depressed for the last eighteen months. Is that a part of his plan as well?"

Shambhu shook his head, "God never wants you to suffer. The suffering is only your perception. Why don't you accept his plans? Accept them, with as much grace as you can. Nothing in this universe happens without a purpose. Everything is a part of the Plan. Your reaction, whether it's joyful or full of sorrow, will have no bearing on the Plan."

Aditya sat silently, trying to absorb the words that his friend was speaking.

Shambhu looked at the clouds above, which were still pouring down raindrops on the earth, "Look at this cloud. It's getting destroyed because it has to rain. After it rains, the cloud will be formed again, in a new shape and colour. Imagine if it resists its destruction, there would be no rain, and the cloud will never be formed again. Getting destroyed and getting formed again is the rule of the universe. To resist it, is to not exist. To accept is to live, to flow, to flourish."

Aditya looked at Shambhu with hopeful eyes, "I want to live, Shambhu! I want to flow; I want to flourish!"

"Then flow, Aditya! Then play, and dance! Then, celebrate every moment. Why did you give up playing? You can achieve all your dreams, without restricting yourself. Study hard, work hard! When you are done studying, then play. If your body becomes static, your mind becomes stagnant too!"

Aditya smiled, with tears in his eyes. "Shambhu, I don't want to grow up. I don't want to get older. Why does my childhood have to be destroyed to create my future? Can't things be good, without destroying them?"

"No Aditya! The force that protects and nourishes, is the force that destroys and creates. A baby is born after destroying blood vessels and the umbilical cord that had been sustaining him for nine months. Surgeries done to save lives also need cutting the skin and muscles. Construction of houses need digging and cutting the ground, wood and mortar. Similarly, the new 'You' cannot emerge unless the old 'You' is destroyed."

"How should I ease the pain of this destruction?" Aditya asked Shambhu.

"There is no point of mourning the inevitable. You can ease the pain by playing and dancing through it. That is the fifth law of happiness—flow and dance through every event of your life."

Shambhu stood up. He kicked the wet, loose mud with his feet, dancing away. Bholu started imitating his master, kicking mud all around him. Aditya laughed, and holding Shambhu's hands, started dancing with him.

Thunder rolled in the sky, as it rained harder. Gusty winds blew through the trees. The air was fragrant with the scent of fresh rain as it soaked the fertile earth.

The universe looked down fondly at the two dancing boys, and their dog as their laughter filled the air around them.

Date: FEBRUARY 24, 2029 | Time: 5.45 PM

Shambhu Departs

It had finally stopped raining. The dark clouds which had been hanging low had been spent and were scattering. The landscape of the sky was painted brilliantly, with multi-hued colors. The birds which had been silent during the rain had started chirping again.

Aditya and Shambhu were sitting under the giant tree, watching the last raindrops falling softly.

"Aditya, it seems that the sun is about to set." Shambhu was looking at the sky.

Aditya remembered the promise that he had made to his mother. It was time for him to get back home.

"Shambhu, I have to go home now. My mother must be waiting for me."

"Yes Aditya, it's time for me to leave as well," Shambhu smiled back.

Aditya felt a wave of affection for his friend. He stood up and held his hands, "Shambhu, I am feeling so happy today! After so many days! So far, my life had been so terrible that I used to feel as I am drinking poison forcefully!"

Shambhu laughed, "C'mon Aditya, there is no poison. That's just your perception again. And whatever it is, why drink it forcefully? You must drink it willingly, with a smile on your face."

"What! Are you crazy? How can anyone drink poison with a smile?" Aditya was aghast.

"No Aditya, I am not crazy. Before I leave, let me tell you one last story. Do you know that Shiva swallowed poison willingly, with a smile on His face?"

"But why? How?" Aditya asked in surprise.

"Aditya, at one time, the Gods started losing all their powers to the demons. There was no peace at all, and mayhem ensued. The lost powers of the Gods could only be restored by drinking the elixir at the bottom of the Kshira Sagar, the Ocean of milk."

"Shambhu, where is this Kshira Sagar located?" Aditya got curious.

He was lost in yet another story that Shambhu was telling. He had forgotten that the sun was setting and he had to get back home.

"Kshira Sagar is a cosmic ocean, located in the heavens. It's a limitless, shining, shimmering, snow white ocean, sparkling with milkiness. Maybe it's the galaxy which you know as the Milky Way in the universe, the Akash Ganga. Perhaps it's invisible and only manifests itself to believers and dreamers."

Aditya was listening to Shambhu, spellbound.

"So, the Gods and Demons started a giant churning of the Milky ocean. So many mystical things appeared due to this churning, Aditya!"

"Like what?" Aditya asked, his mouth open with wonder.

"Fourteen kinds of gems! A wish granting, winged cow with peacock's tail, a white four tusked, seven trunked elephant, a seven headed flying horse, a wish granting, forever flowering tree and many more!"

Aditya's eyes gleamed with delight as he imagined all the beautiful, enchanted creatures rising from the creamy depths of a milky ocean.

Shambhu frowned, "And then came out *halahala*, a pot of the most toxic, lethal poison. It was so poisonous that it had the power to wipe out the entire universe. The Gods approached Lord Shiva and asked him to help the universe from the imminent threat of being destroyed. Do you know what Lord Shiva did?"

Shambhu had a strange glow on his face as Aditya looked perplexed, "What?!"

Shambhu sat up and looked into his eyes, "Aditya, Shiva smiled. He just smiled and drank the poison."

Aditya went silent for a while.

Then he spoke up uncertainly, "Why did you tell me this story, Shambhu?"

Shambhu smiled again, "I told you this story

because your mind is like Kshira Sagar. Every day the positive and negative forces in your mind churn this ocean of your mind, and a thousand thoughts emerge from it. Some are joyful, some are inspiring, some are depressing and some are fearful. Your fears emerge from the depths of your mind, and so do your strengths. And sometimes, just when you feel that elixir will emerge because of your hard work, actually a pot of poison appears!"

"Pot of poison means…," Aditya asked.

"Here, metaphorically, a pot of poison just means hopelessness. The dashing of your dreams! Rejection, and sadness. You have to figuratively drink that poison with a smile, that means you have to take it on the chin bravely, smile and move on. Don't wallow in your despair. Or everything that you have built with your efforts so far will be destroyed. Just have faith, and start again."

Aditya looked up into Shambhu's eyes, his own eyes wet with unshed tears.

Shambhu held Aditya's hand, "And after consuming that pain, Aditya, you will find the elixir that you have been working and striving for. Trust me, my friend, you will find it."

Aditya sat on the wet, green grass, and thought deeply.

Shambhu turned towards him and hugged him tightly, Aditya clung to his friend, hugging him back.

Shambhu looked at him and smiled, "Aditya, my friend, I must leave now because the sun is setting. I have told you all the laws of happiness. You must remember them all your life. Promise me that you will never forget them."

Upon hearing those words, Aditya looked at him with fear in his eyes, "Why Shambhu! Why are you speaking as though we will never meet again? Surely, we will!"

Shambhu smiled again, "You don't have to meet me again to feel my soul. I will always live inside you. I will live through you. I am not limited to any physical form. I am everywhere. I am the mighty winds that blow over the trees. I am also the bright Sun that shines in the blue sky. You will find me in the powerful crashing waves of the ocean. I will come, whenever you call me."

Aditya stood up, looked alarmed, "Are you going away, Shambhu? Please don't! I need you!"

Shambhu stood in front of him, smiling, "Even if I may have to go, do remember that Bholu will always stay with you. Loving him, and receiving his love back, will give you comfort."

He knelt down and whispered something in Bholu's floppy ears.

In response, Bholu barked happily.

Shambhu patted Bholu, who was looking at him with large, trusting eyes. Bholu seemed to understand everything that was being said. He moved closer to

Aditya, nuzzling his furry face near his legs.

"Close your eyes, Aditya!" Shambhu commanded.

Aditya looked at Shambhu for the last time, holding the image of his kind, smiling face in his eyes forever. Then he closed his eyes, as he had to obey his friend.

The next moment, Aditya felt someone calling his name, touching his arm. He tried to ignore that voice, but it was persistent....

"Aditya.... Aditya...."

Date: FEBRUARY 24, 2020 | Time: 6.15 PM

Wake Up, Aditya

"Aditya.... !"

Aditya opened his eyes with a start. He looked around himself, confused and disoriented. He was still sitting on the bench under the gigantic tree.

Shocked, he sprang to his feet, looking around wildly.

His mother was standing next to him, looking at him in obvious concern. Her brow was creased with worry. Aditya realised that it was his mother who had been calling out his name.

Last he remembered; Shambhu had asked him to close his eyes. Now Shambhu was nowhere to be seen!

There was a group of children playing in front of the bench that he had been sitting on. Where had they come from?

The sky was echoing with their happy shouts and laughter. A couple of little puppies were frolicking in delight on the emerald coloured soft, damp grass. It seemed as if it had just rained. The earth was fragrant with the scent of the first drops of rain. Aditya could hear the sound of a flute playing in a distance. Who was playing the flute at this time?

He once again looked at his mother, "Mummy, where is Shambhu?"

"Shambhu? Who is that?" Priyanka looked puzzled.

"My friend Shambhu! Mummy, he was right here!" Aditya's voice was rising as he looked around all over, his eyes searching for his friend.

"There was no one near you. You were sleeping alone on this bench. Were you dreaming of someone?" Priyanka spoke worriedly.

Aditya shook his head, "No Mummy! I wasn't dreaming. I am sure that it was real. Shambhu was real! I had spent the entire day with him, talking, laughing, eating, sleeping and playing with him!"

Aditya realised that he was speaking too fast, in a state of panic. Priyanka was speechless and was just looking at him in surprise, holding his hand.

Aditya pulled his hand from Priyanka's hand and started running helter-skelter, shouting Shambhu's name. The children around him stopped playing and stood there, watching this young teenage boy calling out a name that they had not heard before.

Aditya caught hold of one little boy who was standing awkwardly, "Have you seen a boy wearing a blue shirt and blue jeans?"

The boy looked up at him in alarm, and shook his head, "No!"

Aditya raised his voice and asked the same question from all the children standing around him, "Has any of you seen him?"

All the children stood there mutely, shaking their heads.

No, no one had seen him.

It was getting dark. The green trees that had seemed to shine with raindrops on their leaves, now were looking like dark silhouettes in a distance.

Priyanka walked towards Aditya and held his arm again, "Aditya, you might have been dreaming. No one has seen him. Now come home! It's getting late."

Aditya was reluctant to return home without searching for Shambhu, but he changed his mind after seeing his mother's worried face. He had given enough pain to his mother already. No more!

Aditya took one last look at the bench that he had been sitting on, and the dense trees surrounding it.

All of a sudden, a furry shape came out from the darkness of trees and hurled towards him.

Aditya's heart leapt up with joy.

It was Bholu!

Aditya joyfully yelled Bholu's name as he hugged the friendly dog, who was licking him with affection.

He held the dog close to him as he remembered

Shambhu's words, *"Even if I may have to go, do remember that Bholu will always stay with you."*

"Mummy, meet Bholu! Our dog!" Aditya shouted with joy.

Priyanka smiled affectionately as she stretched her hand and patted Bholu. She felt a sudden joy, seeing her son so happy after many days.

"Let's take him home," Priyanka spoke softly, her voice full of affection for the boy and the dog.

Finally, all three of them walked together, towards their car.

Aditya knew deep down that he will never see Shambhu again.

Yet, he did not feel hopeless.

Shambhu had declared that he will live inside him eternally, like his soul. Aditya will never be alone.

THREE YEARS LATER

Date: October 21, 2032 | Time: 12.28 pm

You're A Skilled Captain, Aditya

The large football stadium was packed with young college students. All the seats were occupied. There was literally no place to even stand. Some students were sitting on the aisles and the steps. After all, this was the most awaited annual football match between St. Soloman's and St Matthew's, the two most prestigious and competitive colleges of the city. The air echoed with loud, youthful cheering. Every time there was a goal, there would be thunderous applause.

"Our passion, our game! Soloman is our name!"

"A cut above the rest! Matthew is the best!"

The noise level was so high that nobody could hear each other. Loud jeering and threats were being exchanged, but most of it was lost in the deafening cacophony.

A minute ago, the commotion reached a peak as the scores of the two teams were now tied. 2-2!!

The time was about to be up in just two minutes.

And the ball was poised beneath the arch of the shoe of St. Soloman's star player, Aditya Kumar.

Nineteen-year-old Aditya stood and looked all around him with the focus and determination of an eagle. As the captain of the Soloman team, he was aware that the entire team had been depending on him to win the match. In fact, some students were surprised that Matthew's team had managed to get an equal score with Aditya being on the opposite team.

However, it had happened, but now there were still two minutes left in the game.

Aditya heard the loud sound of his heart beating over the thunderous sound made by hundreds of students watching him. Everyone's eyes seemed to pierce him like laser beams coming from all directions. He knew that the next two minutes were the most crucial moments for the outcome of the game. If he could score one goal.... just one goal in these two minutes, then his team would win!

As the seconds ticked by, he felt a familiar panic rising inside him. No! He must fight this panic, or he would not be able to score the goal. Yet, that feeling of fear that started at the pit of the football ground was rising alarmingly and threatening to engulf him completely. He felt sweat trickling down his arms, falling down on the earth.

He studied the goal post with as much concentration as he could manage. He saw the goal keeper staring at him with a menacing determination. At a distance, he could hear all his college mates screaming his name.

"Aaaaadityaaaa… doooooo it! Goal! Aaadityaaaa! Gooooaaal!"

To improve his focus, he briefly closed his eyes for a moment. It was no use. It seemed to him as if his fears were literally dancing fiercely on his head.

What if he could not strike the goal? What if his team lost? Everyone will be disappointed in him…

Once more, those fears whispering threateningly in his ears! He was breathing unevenly, in sudden spurts.

All of a sudden, a sense of determination came piercing through the mist of his fears.

Shambhu!

"Shambhu, where are you?" he murmured.

The loud sound of the people in the stadium receded in a distance, till it was gone completely. Everything was silent around him. A quiet peace descended on his soul like a soft cloud over a green mountain.

In that meditative state, he listened to those words in his mind. The words of Shambhu that guided him constantly….

"Take over your ship, Aditya. Tell your fears to leave immediately. Tell them that their time is up. Have faith in yourself, in your life and in your God. You are a skilled captain. Do not forget your own powers. Take a deep breath, and start again."

He took a deep breath, just the way Shambhu had

taught him. Four... Seven... Eight...

Yes!

He felt his power returning to him, coursing down the blood in his veins. He clenched his fist and felt a new vitality crashing down his spirit like a tidal wave. He will not lose!

He opened his eyes and looked at the goal post. The stadium was silent as everyone watched him, not daring to even breathe. His foot arched up, and in an instant, there was a loud, cracking sound as he kicked the ball with all his might. The goal keeper ran from one side to the next, falling over as he tried his best to stop the ball from hitting the post.

But this ball was flying like a missile, and nothing and no one could stop it. Propelled with an invincible force, it hit the goalpost with a resounding thud!

At the same instant, the closing bell sounded. The game was over.

There was a moment of pin drop silence, as everyone tried to process what had just happened. And then the entire stadium burst into the loudest cheer that had never been heard before.

St. Soloman college had won! Aditya had done it!

The students of St. Soloman college rose from their seats like a giant wave in an ocean. Hugging each other with happiness, they ran towards the football ground, falling merrily over each other. Some of them started a victory dance.

Aditya fell on the grass, with his arms outstretched, as his eyes filled up with tears. He did not hear the boisterous yells of his college mates. He was barely aware of his team players falling all over him, in exhilaration of the victory. He was overwhelmed with such powerful emotions that he could no longer contain himself.

His team members lifted him up on their shoulders and danced all the way to the stage where their trophy awaited them. This moment! Where had this moment come from? He looked around him, laughing and crying at the same time.

Date: October 21, 2032 | Time: 2.05 PM

Finale

The match had ended. The trophy received. The last cheer shouted. The last hurrah yelled.

Aditya threw his football gear in his bag, feeling happy. As he was walking out of the stadium, he heard someone calling out his name.

It was Shahid, his best friend, walking towards him. Both the boys shook hands and hugged each other. Next, they both walked together and caught an autorickshaw outside the college to join the rest of the team for a victory lunch.

Aditya was looking out of the autorickshaw dreamily, his hair flying in the wind. He closed his eyes in bliss. He wanted to savour those beautiful moments of success forever.

"Those last moments, bro! I was so scared that I had closed my eyes," Shahid laughed.

Aditya shook his head, "I was so scared too, bro! Seriously!"

"How did you manage it? I would've panicked if I were in your place, I know. So much pressure, dude! One wrong move, and all would've been lost!" Shahid looked at him in wonder.

Aditya became silent as he was lost in his thoughts, "When I am facing my fears, I always remember the words of my friend. That's it. Voila! Those words give me the strength to face just anything!"

"Which friend?" Shahid asked, curiously.

Aditya smiled, "There was someone I met once."

"Only once?" Shahid seemed amazed.

"Yes," Aditya laughed, "Once is enough for a lifelong soul friendship."

As their autorickshaw sped across the city roads, Aditya's eyes were searching for that garden. They were almost there, just across the corner.

And suddenly there it was! The white picket fence, and the dense green trees beckoned him.

"Shahid, could you just drop me right here?" Aditya called out.

"Here? In this garden? But our team is waiting at Shantanu's house. We're already late!" Shahid looked worried as he checked his watch.

"Just ten minutes. Wait for me here, please." Aditya put his hand on Shahid's shoulder.

"Alright, I'm waiting. Come back soon!" Shahid called out.

The next moment, Aditya was running towards the

entrance of the garden.

He passed through the white picket fence and ran down the shaded path. The air instantly felt cooler and fragrant. He kept running till he reached the bench on which he had sat years ago.

He first touched the wooden bench with his strong, firm hands lovingly. Next, he took a deep breath and sat down on it.

At last! At last he was back at the place where he had found the purpose of his soul.

He closed his eyes, inhaling the rich, scented air. He could hear the birds chirping at a distance. He could hear the sonorous sounds of the koel, and the distant song of the peacocks. A squirrel was scurrying about, collecting nuts for its home.

"Shambhu...," he called out.

There was no answer.

He knew that there would be no reply. He had come to this place and called out many times, but he had never met Shambhu again. Shambhu had been true to his word. He had taught him the lessons of life and gone away, confident that Aditya will take care of himself.

Yet, Aditya did not miss him. Whenever he needed him, he could just close his eyes and Shambhu's words would echo in his ears.

"You don't have to meet me again to feel my soul. I will always live inside you. I will live through you. I am

not limited to any physical form. I am everywhere. I am the mighty winds that blow over the trees. I am also the bright Sun that shines in the blue sky. You will find me in the powerful crashing waves of the ocean. I will come, whenever you call me."

Shambhu was everywhere. The conversations with Shambhu were etched in Aditya's soul forever. He was around him, and inside him. He was Aditya's guiding spirit, his beginning, and his end.

Finally, Aditya opened his eyes and stood up. He took a last look at green grass which was spreading from his feet all over the place, like a soft carpet.

All of a sudden, he felt some raindrops falling on his face. He smiled again, "So Shambhu, here you are!" he laughed aloud.

In response, it started raining harder.

Aditya felt as if Shambhu was laughing loudly, shouting in his usual excited way, "Aditya! The earth is dancing. You must dance with it too!"

Aditya laughed back as he ran towards the gate of the garden, in the pouring rain. He had to get back soon, his friends were waiting for him. Bholu was waiting for him.

Life was waiting for him.

Author's Note

Conversations with Shambhu is not merely a book for me. It is a piece of my own heart that I have carved out from the deepest depths of my own phases of depression and self-introspection.

Aditya, the hero of my book, represents all of us, the sensitive, misunderstood souls. He is the hero not because he achieves an award or some external validation, but because he admits that he is depressed and unable to cope and that he needs help.

I am a mother of two evolved souls, Alma and Sitab, who are twenty-four and twenty-three years old respectively. We have had long conversations through the years, all through their highest and lowest points of their lives.

Our conversations were frank, with no topic being taboo amongst us. All the events which have been written in this book are true, which happened to either me or one of them. Such events happen to all of us, and most of the times, we have no one to talk to. At other times, we are told that we must be 'strong', not be 'too sensitive' and simply move on. The truth is that it is not possible to move on from certain traumas that we suffer. We internalise the pain, and pretend that everything is fine, when this is far from the truth.

Our childhoods are idyllic phases where we read fairy tales and watch cartoons of mythical creatures, and so we are all ill-equipped to handle the sudden, cruel shift in our adolescence. All of a sudden, we are forced to grow up overnight and face a competitive world with no help from anyone. We are thrown in a high-pressure environment in which our physical health is tended to but talking about our mental health is frowned upon. Our friends become our rivals and our parents and teachers become our trainers, with whips in their hands.

We all need someone to talk to and someone who empathises with us. We also need yoga and physical exercise to sustain our physical and mental health. The rest of the strength lies within us, and is unleashed the moment we call out to it.

This book is my dedication to all the lonely, beautiful people out there, who need a friend like Shambhu in their lives. Who is Shambhu? That is up to the reader's imagination. Is he a real boy who met Aditya once and then never came back? Is he Lord Shiva? Or is he just an imaginary creation of Aditya's mind? I leave it for you, my dear reader, to decipher that.

We may never find someone like Shambhu, but we can try to be Shambhu in someone's life. What a beautiful world it would be if we all could be there for each other, without passing any judgment.

If you ever want to reach out to me, then drop a mail at : sujatasharma.aiims@gmail.com. I would love to connect with you and listen to your story.